D0501471

The Lover's Dictionary

Farrar, Straus and Giroux   *New York*

The Lover's Dictionary

abyss
anthem antsy
banal beguile better
cadence candid cavort
covet defunct dumbfounded elegy ersatz fast
finances ♡ fluke flux gamut gingerly guise
happenstance healthy hiatus I idea jaded
jerk justice kerfuffle lackluster leery
love macabre misgivings narcissism
obstinate only perfunctory posterity
qualm raze ♡ rest rubberneck
scapegoat serrated suffuse
tableau transient traverse
ubiquitous unabashedly
vestige voluminous
wane whet woo
x yearning
yell

aloof
avant-garde balk
blemish breathtaking
celibacy champagne

DAVID LEVITHAN

Farrar, Straus and Giroux
18 West 18th Street, New York 10011

Copyright © 2011 by David Levithan
All rights reserved
Distributed in Canada by D&M Publishers, Inc.
Printed in the United States of America
First edition, 2011

Library of Congress Control Number: 2010014392
ISBN: 978-0-374-19368-3

Designed by Jonathan D. Lippincott

www.fsgbooks.com

1   3   5   7   9   10   8   6   4   2

For my parents, with gratitude and wonder

The Lover's Dictionary

aberrant, *adj.*

"I don't normally do this kind of thing," you said.

"Neither do I," I assured you.

Later it turned out we had both met people online before, and we had both slept with people on first dates before, and we had both found ourselves falling too fast before. But we comforted ourselves with what we really meant to say, which was: "I don't normally feel this good about what I'm doing."

Measure the hope of that moment, that feeling.

Everything else will be measured against it.

abstain, *v.*

I'm sorry I was so surprised you didn't drink that night.

"Is something wrong?" I asked. It wasn't like you to turn down a drink after work.

"Go ahead," you said. "Drink for both of us."

So I ordered two Manhattans. I didn't know whether to offer you a sip. I didn't know if it could be this easy to get you, for once, to stop.

"What's wrong?" I asked.

After a dramatic pause, you said, totally serious, "I'm pregnant." And then you cracked up.

I laughed even though I didn't feel like laughing. I raised my Manhattan, tipped it a little in your direction, then asked, "Whose is it?"

abstraction, *n.*

Love is one kind of abstraction. And then there are those nights when I sleep alone, when I curl into a pillow that isn't you, when I hear the tiptoe sounds that aren't yours. It's not as if I can conjure you there completely. I must embrace the idea of you instead.

abyss, *n.*

There are times when I doubt everything. When I regret everything you've taken from me, everything I've given you, and the waste of all the time I've spent on us.

acronym, *n.*

I remember the first time you signed an email with SWAK. I didn't know what it meant. It sounded violent, like a slap connecting. SWAK! Batman knocking down the Riddler. SWAK! Cries of "Liar! Liar!" Tears. SWAK! So I wrote back: *SWAK?* And the next time you wrote, ten minutes later, you explained.

I loved the ridiculous image I got from that, of you leaning over your laptop, touching your lips gently to the screen, sealing your words to me before turning them into electricity. Now every time you SWAK me, the echo of that electricity remains.

adamant, *adj.*

You swore that Meryl Streep won the Best Actress Oscar for
Silkwood. I said, no, it was *Sophie's Choice.* The way you ar-
gued with me, you would have thought we were debating the
existence of God or whether or not we should move in together.
These kinds of fights can never be won — even if you're the
victor, you've hurt the other person, and there has to be some
loss associated with that.

We looked it up, of course, and even though you conceded
I was right, you still acted like it was a special occasion. I thought
about leaving you then. Just for a split second, I was out the
door.

akin, *adj.*

I noticed on your profile that you said you loved *Charlotte's Web*. So it was something we talked about on that first date, about how the word *radiant* sealed it for each of us, and how the most heartbreaking moment isn't when Charlotte dies, but when it looks like all of her children will leave Wilbur, too.

In the long view, did it matter that we shared this? Did it matter that we both drank coffee at night and both happened to go to Barcelona the summer after our senior year? In the long view, was it such a revelation that we were both ticklish and that we both liked dogs more than cats? Really, weren't these facts just placeholders until the long view could truly assert itself?

We were painting by numbers, starting with the greens. Because that happened to be our favorite color. And this, we figured, had to mean something.

alfresco, *adv.*

We couldn't stand the city one minute longer, so we walked right into the rent-a-car place, no reservation, and started our journey upstate. As you drove, I called around, and eventually I found us a cabin. We stopped at a supermarket and bought a week's worth of food for two nights.

It wasn't too cold out, so we moved the kitchen table outside. The breeze kept blowing out the candles, but that didn't matter, because for the first time in our relationship, there were plenty of stars above us.

The wine set the tone of our conversation — languid, tipsy, earthy.

"I love dining alfresco," you said, and I laughed a little.

"What?" you asked.

And I said, "We're not naked, silly."

Now it was your turn to laugh.

"That's not what it means," you told me. "And anyway, don't you feel naked now?"

You fell quiet, gestured for me to listen. The sound of the woods, the feel of the air. The wine settling in my thoughts. The sky, so present. And you, watching me take it all in.

Naked to the world. The world, naked to us.

aloof, *adj.*

It has always been my habit, ever since junior high school, to ask that question:

"What are you thinking?"

It is always an act of desperation, and I keep on asking, even though I know it will never work the way I want it to.

anachronism, *n.*

"I'll go get the horse and buggy," you'll say.

And I'll say, "But I thought we were taking the hovercraft!"

anthem, *n.*

It was our sixth (maybe seventh) date. I had cooked and you had insisted on doing the dishes. You wouldn't even let me dry. Then, when you were done, smelling of suds, you sat back down and I poured you another glass of cheapish wine. You put your legs in my lap and slouched as if we'd just had a feast for thousands and you'd been the only chambermaid on duty to clean it up.

There was a pause. I was still scared by every gap in our conversation, fearing that this was it, the point where we had nothing left to say. I was still trying to impress you, and I still wanted to be impressed by you, so I could pass along pieces of your impressiveness in stories to my friends, convincing myself this was possible.

"If you were a country," I said, "what would your national anthem be?"

I meant a pre-existing song — "What a Wonderful World" or "Que Sera, Sera" or something to make it a joke, like "Hey Ya!" ("I would like, more than anything else, for my nation to be shaken like a Polaroid picture.")

But instead you said, "It would have to be a blues song." And then you looked up at the ceiling, closed your eyes, and began to sing a blues riff:

Nuh-nah-nuh-nuh
My work makes me tired

Nuh-nah-nuh-nuh
But I gotta pay my rent
Nuh-nah-nuh-nuh
My parents never loved me
Nuh-nah-nuh-nuh
Left all my emotions bent
Nuh-nah-nuh-nuh
I know what I'm here for
Nuh-nah-nuh-nuh
Make your dishes so clean
Nuh-nah-nuh-nuh
Just be careful what you wish for
Nuh-nah-nuh-nuh
'Cause most my shit is unseen
Nuh-nah-nuh-nuh
So many men
Nuh-nah-nuh-nuh
Fall into my trap
Nuh-nah-nuh-nuh
But, boy, I gotta tell you
Nuh-nah-nuh-nuh
You might rewrite that map
Nuh-nah-nuh-nuh
Because I'm a proud nation
Nuh-nah-nuh-nuh
It's written here on my flag
Nuh-nah-nuh-nuh
It's a fucked-up world, boy
Nuh-nah-nuh-nuh
So you better make me laugh

Then you stopped and opened your eyes to me. I applauded.

"Don't sit there clapping," you said. "Rub this blues singer's feet."

You never asked what my anthem was. But that's okay, because I still don't know what I'd answer.

antiperspirant, *n.*

"There is nothing attractive about smelling like baking powder," I said.

"Baking *soda*," you corrected.

"So if I want to make a pound cake, I can throw some butter, flour, and sugar into your armpit —"

"Why are we having this conversation? Remind me again?"

"You no longer smell the yeasty goodness that you apply under your arms, because you are completely used to it. I, however, feel like I am dating a Whole Foods."

"Fine," you said.

I was surprised. "'Fine'?"

"Let the record show, I have stepped onto the slippery slope of compromise in the name of promoting peace and harmony. There will be a ceremonial burning of the deodorant in ten minutes. I hope it's flammable."

"It's just that I really hate it," I told you.

"Well, I hate your toe hair."

"I'll wear socks," I promised. "All the time. Even in the shower."

"Just be warned," you said. "Someday you'll ask me to give up something I really love, and then it's going to get ugly."

antsy, *adj.*

I swore I would never take you to the opera again.

arcane, *adj.*

It was Joanna who noticed it first. We were over at her house for dinner, and she said something about being able to see the woman across the street doing yoga in the mornings, and how strange it looked when you were watching it from a distance.

"So how *is* Miss Torso doing?" you asked.

And I said, "Perhaps we should ask the pianist."

Joanna just looked at us and said, "It used to be that you each had your own strange, baffling references. Now you have them together."

People often say that when couples are married for a long time, they start to look alike. I don't believe that. But I do believe their sentences start to look alike.

ardent, *adj.*

It was after sex, when there was still heat and mostly breathing, when there was still touch and mostly thought . . . it was as if the whole world could be reduced to the sound of a single string being played, and the only thing this sound could make me think of was you. Sometimes desire is air; sometimes desire is liquid. And every now and then, when everything else is air and liquid, desire solidifies, and the body is the magnet that draws its weight.

arduous, *adj.*

Sometimes during sex, I wish there was a button on the small of your back that I could press and cause you to be done with it already.

arrears, *n.*

My faithfulness was as unthinking as your lapse. Of all the things I thought would go wrong, I never thought it would be that.

"It was a mistake," you said. But the cruel thing was, it felt like the mistake was mine, for trusting you.

autonomy, *n.*

"I want my books to have their own shelves," you said, and that's how I knew it would be okay to live together.

avant-garde, *adj.*

This was after Alisa's show, the reverse-blackface rendition of *Gone With the Wind*, including songs from the *Empire Records* soundtrack and an interval of nineteenth-century German poetry, recited with a lisp.

"What does *avant-garde* mean, anyway?" I asked.

"I believe it translates as *favor to your friends*," you replied.

awhile, *adv.*

I love the vagueness of words that involve time.

It took him awhile to come back — it could be a matter of minutes or hours, days or years.

It is easy for me to say it took me awhile to know. That is about as accurate as I can get. There were sneak previews of knowing, for sure. Instances that made me feel, oh, this could be right. But the moment I shifted from a hope that needed to be proven to a certainty that would be continually challenged? There's no pinpointing that.

Perhaps it never happened. Perhaps it happened while I was asleep. Most likely, there's no signal event. There's just the steady accumulation of *awhile*.

B

balk, *v.*

I was the one who said we should live together. And even as I was doing it, I knew this would mean that I would be the one to blame if it all went wrong. Then I consoled myself with this: if it all went wrong, the last thing I'd care about was who was to blame for moving in together.

banal, *adj.*, and **bane**, *n.*

I am interested in the connection between these two words, and how one denotes the series of ordinary spirit-deaths that occur during a day, while the other is the full ruination, the core of the calamity.

    I think we endure the banal —

    "So how's your chicken?"

    "I'm so tired."

    "Lord, it's cold."

    "Where were you?"

    "Where do you want to go?"

    "Have you been waiting long?"

    — as a way of skirting around the bane.

barfly, *n.*

You have the ability to talk to anyone, which is an ability I do
not share.

basis, *n.*

There has to be a moment at the beginning when you wonder whether you're in love with the person or in love with the
feeling of love itself.

If the moment doesn't pass, that's it — you're done.

And if the moment *does* pass, it never goes that far. It
stands in the distance, ready for whenever you want it back.
Sometimes it's even there when you thought you were search-
ing for something else, like an escape route, or your lover's
face.

beguile, *v.*

It's when you walk around the apartment in my boxers when you don't know I'm awake. And then that grin, when you do know I'm awake. You spend so much time in the morning making sure every hair is in place. But I have to tell you: I like it most like this, haphazard, sleep-strewn, disarrayed.

belittle, *v.*

No, I don't listen to the weather in the morning. No, I don't keep track of what I spend. No, it hadn't occurred to me that the Q train would have been much faster. But every time you give me that look, it doesn't make me want to live up to your standards.

bemoan, *v.*

This is dedicated to your co-worker Marilynn.

Marilynn, please stop talking about your sister's pregnancy.

And please stop showing up late.

And please stop asking my lover to drinks.

And please stop humming while you type.

I'm tired of hearing about it.

better, *adj.* and *adv.*

Will it ever get better?
    It better.
    Will it ever get better?
    It better.
    Will it ever get better?
    It better.

beware, *v.*

"My worse date ever?" I asked. "I don't know. I'm always amazed when the other person doesn't ask you anything about yourself. This one date — once the autobiography started, it wouldn't stop. I actually sat there, thinking, *Wow, you're not going to ask me a single question, are you?* And sure enough. Ten minutes. Thirty minutes. An hour. Only one subject. And it wasn't me."

"So, what did you do?" you asked.

"I just started counting. Like sheep. And when the waiter asked if we wanted to have dessert, my date started to order, and I interrupted and said I had promised a friend to walk his dog. What about you?"

"It's embarrassing."

"Tell me!"

"Okay. It was a set-up. And the minute I saw him, I was like — the attraction level was in the deep negatives. Like, I've seen sexier tree stumps. But of course you can't say that. I tried to be a better person. Then he opened his mouth and I was completely repulsed. Not only did he talk about himself all night, but he also kept cutting me off whenever I had an opinion about anything. The worst part was: I could see he was enjoying himself! So — God, I'm not proud of this. In fact, I can't believe I'm telling you this. You promise you won't think I'm a freak?"

"I won't."

"Okay. So there'd been this fly hovering over our table. I kept trying to shoo it with my hand. After awhile I was focusing on the fly more than the guy. He was getting annoyed. So the next time it came close to my face I just . . . stuck out my tongue."

"Like you were a frog?"

You nodded. "Like I was a frog."

"And you caught the fly."

"Yup. Swallowed it down. It was worth it to see the look on his face. Dessert wasn't an option after that. And I was so relieved. With all due respect to the fly and its right to live, it was completely worth it."

At that point the waiter came over and asked if we needed anything else.

And you said, "I think we're going to get another round of dessert."

blemish, *n.*

The slight acne scars. The penny-sized, penny-shaped birthmark right above your knee. The dot below your shoulder that must have been from when you had chicken pox in third grade. The scratch on your neck — did I do that?

This brief transcript of moments, written on the body, is so deeply satisfying to read.

bolster, *v.*

I am very careful whenever I know you're on the phone with
your father. I know you'll come to me eventually, and we'll
talk you through it. But I have to wait — you need your time.
In the meantime, I'm careful what songs I play. I try to speak
to you with my selections.

brash, *adj.*

"I want you to spend the night," you said. And it was definitely your phrasing that ensured it. If you had said, "Let's
have sex," or "Let's go to my place," or even "I really want you,"
I'm not sure we would have gone quite as far as we did. But
I loved the notion that the night was mine to spend, and I
immediately decided to spend it on you.

breach, *n.*

I didn't want to know who he was, or what you did, or that it didn't mean anything.

breathing, *n.*

You had asthma as a child, had to carry around an inhaler. But when you grew older, it went away. You could run for miles and it was fine.

Sometimes I worry that this is happening to me in reverse. The older I get, the more I lose my ability to breathe.

breathtaking, *adj.*

Those mornings when we kiss and surrender for an hour before we say a single word.

broker, *n.* and *v.*

You knew I was lazy, so you'd be the one to find the apartment. And I played along, partly because I didn't know how you'd react if I called one afternoon and said, "You won't believe the place I've found." You wanted to be the finder, so I became the second opinion.

The brokers nearly broke you. I thought it was sweet and almost sad how desperately you clung to the hope of finding civility — even enthusiasm — in the New York City real estate market. But leave it to you, ten days into the soul-draining hunt, to find not only a decent apartment but a broker we'd end up becoming friends with. By the time I got there, you'd already decided. And I quickly decided to let you decide. You were already seeing the rooms as ours, and that was enough for me.

Well, that and a dishwasher.

buffoonery, *n.*

You were drunk, and I made the mistake of mentioning *Showgirls* in a near-empty subway car. The pole had no idea what it was about to endure.

C

cache, *n.*

I decided to clean my desk. I had thought you were busy in the kitchen. But then I heard you behind me, heard you ask:

"What's in the folder?"

I'm sure I blushed when I told you they were printouts of your emails, with letters and notes from you pressed between them, like flowers in a dictionary.

You didn't say anything more, and I was grateful.

cadence, *n.*

I have never lived anywhere but New York or New England, but there are times when I'm talking to you and I hit a Southern vowel, or a word gets caught in a Southern truncation, and I know it's because I'm swimming in your cadences, that you permeate my very language.

cajole, *v.*

I didn't understand how someone from a completely land-locked state could be so terrified of sharks. Even in the aquarium, I had to do everything to get you to come close to the tank. Then, in the Natural History Museum, I couldn't stay quiet any longer.

"It's not alive," I said. "It can't hurt you."

But you held back, and I was compelled to push you into the glass.

What did it matter to me? Did I think that by making you rational about one thing, I could make you rational about everything?

Maybe. Or maybe I just wanted to save you from your fears.

candid, *adj.*

"Most times, when I'm having sex, I'd rather be reading."

This was, I admit, a strange thing to say on a second date. I guess I was just giving you warning.

"Most times when I'm reading," you said, "I'd rather be having sex."

canvas, *n.*

We both missed our apartments, that first night, but I think you were the one who came closer to genuine regret. I'm sure if we could have afforded it, we would have kept both places. But instead, there we were, in three rooms of our own, which didn't feel like our own, not yet. You wanted me to think you were asleep, but I caught you staring at the ceiling.

"It will be different once we paint," I promised. "It will be different when we put things on the walls."

catalyst, *n.*

It surprised me — surprises me still — that you were the first one to say it.

I was innocent, in a way, expecting those three words to appear boldface with music. But instead, it was such an ordinary moment: The movie was over, and I stood up to turn off the TV. A few minutes had passed from the end of the final credits, and we'd been sitting there on the couch, your legs over mine, the side of your hand touching the side of my hand. The video stopped and the screen turned blue. "I'll get it," I said, and was halfway to the television when you said, "I love you."

I never asked, but I'll always wonder: What was it about that moment that made you realize it? Or, if you'd known it for awhile, what compelled you to say it then? It was welcome, so welcome, and in my rush to say that I loved you, too, I left the television on, I let that light bathe us for a little longer, as I returned to the couch, to you. We held there for awhile, not really sure what would happen next.

catharsis, *n.*

I took it out on the wall.

I LOVE YOU. I LOVE YOU. YOU FUCKER, I LOVE YOU.

caveat, *n.*

"I will be the one to leave you" — you whispered it to me as a warning. Fifth date? Sixth date?

I was sure in my heart that you were wrong. I was sure I'd be the one to kill it. But I kept that belief to myself.

cavort, *v.*

"It's way too late to go into Central Park," I protested.

"The moon is out," you said.

"We really shouldn't."

"Don't worry," you told me, taking my hand. "I'll protect you."

I had always been afraid of walking through the park at night, but soon there we were, well past midnight in the middle of the Great Lawn, having all that space to ourselves, feeling free enough to make out, but trying to keep on as much clothing as possible. Laughing at our recklessness, feeling the grass and the dirt as we rolled playfully — me on top, then you on top, then me on top — zippers down, hands everywhere — night on skin and such nervousness. We sensed people coming closer and got ourselves back together, riding the excitement until the excitement ended, then gliding on a little farther, buoyed not by thrill but by happiness.

celibacy, *n.*

n/a

champagne, *n.*

You appear at the foot of the bed with a bottle of champagne, and I have no idea why. I search my mind desperately for an occasion I've forgotten — is this some obscure anniversary or, even worse, a not-so-obscure one? Then I think you have something to tell me, some good news to share, but your smile is silent, cryptic. I sit up in bed, ask you what's going on, and you shake your head, as if to say that nothing's going on, as if to pretend that we usually start our Wednesday mornings with champagne.

You touch the bottle to my leg — I feel the cool condensation and the glass, the fact that the bottle must have been sleeping all night in the refrigerator without me noticing. You have long-stemmed glasses in your other hand, and you place them on the nightstand, beside the uncommenting clock, the box of Kleenex, the tumbler of water.

"The thing about champagne," you say, unfoiling the cork, unwinding its wire restraint, "is that it is the ultimate associative object. Every time you open a bottle of champagne, it's a celebration, so there's no better way of starting a celebration than opening a bottle of champagne. Every time you sip it, you're sipping from all those other celebrations. The joy accumulates over time."

You pop the cork. The bubbles rise. I feel some of the spray on my skin. You pour.

"But why?" I ask as you hand me my glass.

You raise yours and ask, "Why not? What better way to start the day?"

We drink a toast to that.

circuitous, *adj.*

We do not divulge our histories chronologically. It's not like we can sit each other down and say, "Tell me what happened," and then rise from that conversation knowing everything. Most of the time, we don't even realize that we're dividing ourselves into clues. You'll say, "That was before my dad left my mom," and I'll say, "Your dad left your mom?" Or I'll say, "That was right before Jamie told me we should just be friends," and you'll ask, "Who's Jamie?" I'll swear Jamie was on that initial roll call of heartbreak (perfect for any second date), but maybe I forgot, or maybe you've forgotten. I swear I told you I was allergic to sunflowers. You might have told me your sister once pulled out a handful of your hair, and you were both terrified when your scalp bled. But I don't think you did. I think I'd remember that.

Tell me again.

clandestine, *adj.*

Some familiarity came easy — letting myself laugh even though I guffaw, sharing my shortcomings, walking around the apartment naked. And some intimacy came eventually — peeing in the toilet while you are right there in the shower, or finishing something you've half eaten. But no matter how I try, I still can't write in my journal when you're in the room. It's not even that I'm writing about you (although often I am). I just need to know that nobody's reading over my shoulder, about to ask me what I'm writing. I want to sequester this one part of me from everyone else. I want the act to be a secret, even if the words can only hold themselves secret for so long.

cocksure, *adj.*

We walk into a bar, and you're aware of all the eyes on you.

We walk into a bar, and I'm aware of all the eyes on you, too.

For you, this translates into confidence. But me?

All I can feel is doubt.

commonplace, *adj.*

It swings both ways, really.

I'll see your hat on the table and I'll feel such longing for you, even if you're only in the other room. If I know you aren't looking, I'll hold the green wool up to my face, inhale that echo of your shampoo and the cold air from outside.

But then I'll walk into the bathroom and find you've forgotten to put the cap back on the toothpaste again, and it will be this splinter that I just keep stepping on.

community, *n.*

You feel like you're getting to know all the people on the dating site. It's the same faces over and over again. You can leave for a year and then come back, and they're all waiting for you. Same screennames with the same photos looking for the same things. Only the age has changed, mechanically adjusted as if it's the only thing that's passing. If you've gone on bad dates, they're still there. If you've gone on good dates that eventually didn't work out, they're still there. You cancel your subscription. You sign back up. You think this time will be different.

It's demoralizing and intriguing and sometimes sexy and mostly boring. It's what you do late at night, when your brain has given up on all the other things it has to do — relationship porn. You scroll through. How genius to call them thumbnails, because what part of the body tells us less? (And yet, this is how I find you.)

Every now and then it would happen: I would see someone from the site on the subway, or on the street, or in a bar. A fellow member of the community, out in the real world. I'd want to say, "Don't I know you from somewhere?" And I'd want to say, "Don't I know you from nowhere?" But ultimately I wouldn't say a word. I wasn't sure I wanted them to be real.

composure, *n.*

You told me anyway, even though I didn't want to know. A stupid drunken fling while you were visiting Toby in Austin. Months ago. And the thing I hate the most is knowing how much hinges on my reaction, how your unburdening can only lead to me being burdened. If I lose it now, I will lose you, too. I know that. I hate it.

You wait for my response.

concurrence, *n.*

We eventually discovered that we had both marched in the same Macy's Thanksgiving Day Parade. Your first time in New York, feeling like you were marching through canyons, the skyscrapers leaning over to peek down at you and your trombone. Me, farther back, crashing the cymbals together, preparing my smile for the minute we'd be on TV. What if Katie Couric had turned to me and said, "The love of your life is here in this crowd"? Would I have believed her? Would it have even been possible, if we'd met then?

confluence, *n.*

The first time our mothers met: my birthday, our apartment.
My father, your sister, her kids. How unreal it seemed at first —
unreal and forced. It's one thing to share kisses and secrets
and sex and a bed. But sharing families marks the meeting
of the rivers. I think it was my dad and your niece who bonded
first, over Chutes and Ladders. I can remember how thankful
I felt for that one small interaction. My mother tried; yours,
not so much. We kept talking and talking, filling the room
with words, trying to make a party out of our voices.

contiguous, *adj.*

I felt silly for even mentioning it, but once I did, I knew I had to explain.

"When I was a kid," I said, "I had this puzzle with all fifty states on it — you know, the kind where you have to fit them all together. And one day I got it in my head that California and Nevada were in love. I told my mom, and she had no idea what I was talking about. I ran and got those two pieces and showed it to her — California and Nevada, completely in love. So a lot of the time when we're like this" — my ankles against the backs of your ankles, my knees fitting into the backs of your knees, my thighs on the backs of your legs, my stomach against your back, my chin folding into your neck — "I can't help but think about California and Nevada, and how we're a lot like them. If someone were drawing us from above as a map, that's what we'd look like; that's how we are."

For a moment, you were quiet. And then you nestled in and whispered,

"*Contiguous.*"

And I knew you understood.

corrode, *v.*

I spent all this time building a relationship. Then one night
I left the window open, and it started to rust.

covet, *v.*

This is a difference between us: you desire what other people have, while I desire the things I used to have, or think I might have one day.

Sometimes, with you, it's stupid things. Like shoes. Or a bigger-screen TV, like the one we see at someone's apartment. Or a share in the Hamptons, even though we can't afford a share in the Hamptons and would hate it there.

But every now and then I'm caught off guard. Like when we're over at my cousin's house and her kids are running everywhere. Her husband brings her coffee without her asking for it. They seem exhausted, but you can tell the exhaustion is worth it. And the kids — the kids are happy. They are so happy on such a base level that they don't seem to understand that it's possible to have anything other than a base level of happiness. I catch you desiring that. For your past? For your present? Your future? I have no idea. I never know what you really want, if I can give it to you, or if I'm already too late.

D

daunting, *adj.*

Really, we should use this more as a verb. You daunted me, and I daunted you. Or would it be that I was daunted by you, and you were daunted by me? That sounds better. It daunted me that you were so beautiful, that you were so at ease in social situations, as if every room was heliotropic, with you at the center. And I guess it daunted you that I had so many more friends than you, that I could put my words together like this, on paper, and could sometimes conjure a certain sense out of things.

The key is to never recognize these imbalances. To not let the dauntingness daunt us.

deadlock, *n.*

Just when it would seem like we were at a complete stand-still, the tiebreakers would save us.

If Emily's birthday party and Evan's birthday party were on the same night, we'd go to the movies instead of having to choose. If I wanted Mexican and you wanted Italian, we'd take it as a sign to go for Thai. If I wanted to get back to New York and you wanted to spend another night in Boston, we'd find a bed-and-breakfast somewhere in between. Even if neither of us got what we wanted, we found freedom in the third choices.

deciduous, *adj.*

I couldn't believe one person could own so many shoes, and still buy new ones every year.

defunct, *adj.*

You brought home a typewriter for me.

detachment, *n.*

I still don't know if this is a good quality or a bad one, to be able to be in the moment and then step out of it. Not just during sex, or while talking, or kissing. I don't deliberately pull away — I don't think I do — but I find myself suddenly there on the outside, unable to lose myself in where I am. You catch me sometimes. You'll say I'm drifting off, and I'll apologize, trying to snap back to the present.

But I should say this:

Even when I detach, I care. You can be separate from a thing and still care about it. If I wanted to detach completely, I would move my body away. I would stop the conversation midsentence. I would leave the bed. Instead, I hover over it for a second. I glance off in another direction. But I always glance back at you.

disabuse, *v.*

I love the idea that an abuse can be negated. And that the things most often disabused are notions.

disarray, *n.*

At times, I feel like I'm living with a ninety-year-old, finding a box of crackers in the laundry hamper, or a pair of socks by the vodka. Sometimes I tell you where I found things, and we joke about it. Other times, I just put them back.

dispel, *v.*

It was the way you said, "I have something to tell you." I could feel the magic drain from the room.

dissonance, *n.*

Nights when I need to sleep and you can't. Days when I want to talk and you won't. Hours when every noise you make interferes with my silence. Weeks when there is a buzzing in the air, and we both pretend we don't hear it.

doldrums, *n.*

The proper verb for *depression* is *sink*.

dumbfounded, *adj.*

And still, for all the jealousy, all the doubt, sometimes I will be struck with a kind of awe that we're together. That someone like me could find someone like you — it renders me wordless. Because surely words would conspire against such luck, would protest the unlikelihood of such a turn of events.

I didn't tell any of my friends about our first date. I waited until after the second, because I wanted to make sure it was real. I wouldn't believe it had happened until it had happened again. Then, later on, I would be overwhelmed by the evidence, by all the lines connecting you to me, and us to love.

ebullient, *adj.*

I once told Amanda, my best friend in high school, that I could never be with someone who wasn't excited by rainstorms. So when the first one came, it was a kind of test. It was one of those sudden storms, and when we left Radio City, we found hundreds of people skittishly sheltered under the overhang.

"What should we do?" I asked.

And you said, "Run!"

So that's what we did — rocketing down Sixth Avenue, dashing around the rest of the post-concert crowd, splashing our tracks until our ankles were soaked. You took the lead, and I started to lose my sprint. But then you looked back, stopped, and waited for me to catch up, for me to take your hand, for us to continue to run in the rain, drenched and enchanted, my words to Amanda no longer feeling like a requirement, but a foretelling.

elegy, *n.*

Your grandfather dies a few months after we move in together. There is no question that I will go with you, but there are plenty of questions when we get to the funeral. I know you haven't slept. I know you've spent the night on the computer, trying to pin down what you feel. I know why you didn't accept my offer to help, just as you know why I felt I had to offer it anyway. On the car ride down, you practice what you're going to say. You use the word *confliction* when you really should just say *conflict*, and you use the word *remarkability*, which I'm not sure is even a word. But I don't say a thing — I just listen to you say them over and over again, because they are what you need to say.

Then we get there, and the first words out of your mother's mouth are "Nobody's speaking at the service." That, more than anything else, throws you off, makes it seem like you've been bequeathed a bad patch of gravity. I'm bombarded from all sides — most people don't know my name, and nobody knows what to call me in relation to you. Something more than a boyfriend, something less than a spouse. I met your grandfather once, and he was nice to me. That's what I can contribute — that I met your grandfather once, and that he was nice to me.

Something happens to us that day. It's there during the service, when you don't let go of my hand. It's there back at your mother's house, where we retreat to your childhood bedroom and go through your old chest of drawers, where we find stale jellybeans and notes from high school you hadn't wanted your mother to unearth. It's there when your mother bursts into tears after most of the guests have gone, and I don't need you to say a word to know I am not to leave the room until you're leaving it with me. We have fallen through the surface of want and are deep in the trenches of need.

That night, driving home, I ask you to tell me stories about your grandfather, and as we travel farther and farther from your mother's house and closer and closer to our own apartment, you unspool the memories and turn them into words. From behind the wheel, I learn the difference between a eulogy and an elegy, and discover which is more vital, in life and in death.

elliptical, *adj.*

The kiss I like the most is one of the slow ones. It's as much breath as touch, as much *no* as *yes*. You lean in from the side, and I have to turn a little to make it happen.

encroach, *v.*

The first three nights we spent together, I couldn't sleep. I wasn't used to your breathing, your feet on my legs, your weight in the bed. In truth, I still sleep better when I'm alone. But now I allow that sleep isn't always the most important thing.

ephemeral, *adj.*

I was coming back from the bathroom. You had just checked your email. I was walking to bed, but you intercepted me, kissed me, then clasped my left hand in your right hand and put your left hand on my back. We started slow-dancing. No music, just nighttime. You leaned your head into mine and I leaned my head into yours. *Dancing cheek to cheek.* Revolving slowly, eyes closed, heartbeat measure, nature's hum. It lasted the length of an old song, and then we stopped, kissed, and the world resumed.

epilogue, *n.*

You walk into the doorway just as I'm about to finish. You ask
me what I'm writing.

"You'll see," I say. "I promise."

These words are now mine, but soon they'll be ours.

epithet, *n.*

I think the worst you ever called me was a "cunt rag."

"You mean I'm a *tampon?*" I asked. "I'm a *tampon* for not letting you drive?"

I laughed. You didn't. At least, not until you sobered up.

ersatz, *adj.*

Sometimes we'd go to a party and I would feel like an artificial boyfriend, a placeholder, a boyfriend-shaped space where a charming person should be. Those were the only times when my love for you couldn't overcome my shyness. And every degree of disappointment I'd feel from you — whether real or of my own invention — would make me disappear further and further, leaving the fake front to nod, to sip, to say, "Finish your drink, we're leaving."

ethereal, *adj.*

You leaned your head into mine, and I leaned my head into yours. *Dancing cheek to cheek.* Revolving slowly, eyes closed, heartbeat measure, nature's hum. It lasted the length of an old song, and then we stopped, kissed, and my heart stayed there, just like that.

exacerbate, *v.*

I believe your exact words were: "You're getting too emotional."

exemplar, *n.*

It's always something we have to negotiate — the fact that my parents are happy, and yours have never been. I have something to live up to, and if I fail, I still have a family to welcome me home. You have a storyline to rewrite, and a lack of faith that it can ever be done.

You love my parents, I know. But you never get too close. You never truly believe there aren't bad secrets underneath.

fabrication, *n.*

In my online profile, I had lied about my age. Only by two years — I don't even know why. I changed it to my real age the morning after our first date. If you noticed the incongruity, you never mentioned it.

fallible, *adj.*

I was hurt. Of course I was hurt. But in a perverse way, I was
relieved that you were the one who made the mistake. It made
me worry less about myself.

fast, *n.* and *adj.*

Starvation and speed. Noun and adjective. This is where I get caught. A fast is the opposite of desire. It is the negation of desire. It is what I feel after we fight.

The speed does us in. We act rashly, we say too much, we don't let all the synapses connect before we do the thing we shouldn't do.

You make it a production. Slam doors. Knock things over. Scream. But I just leave. Even if I'm still standing there, I leave. I am refusing you. I am denying you. I am an adjective that is quickly turning into a noun.

finances, *n.*

You wanted to keep the list on the refrigerator.

"No," I said. "That's too public."

What I meant was: *Aren't you embarrassed by how much you owe me?*

flagrant, *adj.*

I would be standing right there, and you would walk out of
the bathroom without putting the cap back on the toothpaste.

fledgling, *adj.*

Part of the reason I preferred reading to sex was that I at least knew I could read well. It took your patience to allow me to like it more. And eventually I even stopped seeing it as patience.

fluke, *n.*

The date before the one with you had gone so badly — egotist,
smoker, bad breath — that I'd vowed to delete my profile the
next morning. Except when I went to do it, I realized I only
had eight days left in the billing cycle. So I gave it eight days.
You emailed me on the sixth.

flux, *n.*

The natural state. Our moods change. Our lives change. Our feelings for each other change. Our bearings change. The song changes. The air changes. The temperature of the shower changes.

Accept this. We must accept this.

fraught, *adj.*

Does every "I love you" deserve an "I love you too"? Does every kiss deserve a kiss back? Does every night deserve to be spent on a lover?

If the answer to any of these is "No," what do we do?

G

gamut, *n.*

When I was eight, I was the lead in our third-grade musical, a truncated version of *The Sound of Music* featuring only the numbers in which the Von Trapp children appeared. I was Kurt, and my whole family — grandparents, aunts, uncles, parents, even some family friends — showed up to see me bid *adieu, adieu* to *you and you and you.* My mother took hundreds of pictures, one of which found its way to our apartment — me in a green floral shirt, meant to approximate curtains. I am smiling, so proud of myself and my role.

You saw this and told me that when you were eight, you were a tree in the school play. You can't remember the name of the play, or the story. Only the cardboard branches that you cut out yourself, because your mom was busy and your father didn't think it was his job to help you. They promised they would come, but your mother ran late and your father said he forgot. That night, you tore up your costume into tiny little pieces, but nobody noticed. You scattered the cardboard in the forest on your way to school the next day. You can't remember what the play was about, but you can remember the sight of the trail you left.

gingerly, *adj.*

Your grandmother dies a few weeks after we start seeing each other, and there is no question that you'll go to the funeral without me. Your father calls to tell you while we're having breakfast, and keeps the conversation short. I take you home, help you pack, help you book your ticket. You won't cry, and that makes me want to. I take the subway with you to the airport, even though you tell me I don't have to. Then I stay home and wait for you to call. I cancel my plans, keep the ringer on high. The minute you're alone, you call me, and I talk to you for five long hours, tethering you to your life back here so you won't be pulled back into theirs. I don't comment on your lack of tears, but then you bring it up, say, "I guess I'm so used to a dying family that this doesn't seem out of the ordinary."

You leave the phone on beside you as you fall asleep. I sit in my bed and listen to your breathing, until I know you are safe, until I know you no longer need me for the night.

gravity, *n.*

I imagine you saved my life. And then I wonder if I'm just imagining it.

gregarious, *adj.*

Soon I was able to measure the alcohol and its effect.

One drink and you'd unwind a little, and always order another.

Two drinks and you were happily unsettled. You'd loosen or lose a layer of clothing. You'd talk effortlessly with our friends.

Three drinks and you started to get going. Encouraging everyone else to drink. Joking around with me, if you could tell I was in the mood to joke. Talking to strangers. Saying you loved life.

Four drinks and you stopped reading my cues. You joked regardless of my mood, sometimes mercilessly. Everyone was now your friend, except maybe me.

Five drinks and you were the funniest person you'd ever heard, and you were charismatic enough to make everyone else believe it, too. Sometimes, at this point, you'd tell everyone how much you loved me. Or you'd ignore me.

Six drinks and you were ready to fall.

Of course, it would all depend on the drink. But eventually I learned to take that into account, too.

I would always wait to take you home.

grimace, *n.*

Yes, I keep the water next to the bed in case I get thirsty at night. But it's also for the morning, so you can take a sip before you kiss me.

guise, *n.*

It was a slow Sunday. You were reading the paper, and I was cleaning up after breakfast. The light between the slats of the blinds was making your hair glow in a pattern that shifted every time you moved. You sensed me watching, looked up.

"What?" you asked.

"I just wonder," I said. "How do you picture yourself?"

You looked down at the paper, then back at me.

"I don't know," you said. "I don't ever really see myself. And when I do, I'm usually still an eighteen-year-old, wondering what the hell I'm doing. You?"

And I told you: I think of a photograph you took of me, up in Montreal. You told me to jump in the air, so in the picture, my feet are off the ground. Later, I asked you why you wanted me to do that, and you told me it was the only way to get me to forget about the expression on my face. You were right. I am completely unposed, completely genuine. In my mind's eye, I picture myself like that, reacting to you.

halcyon, *adj.*

A snow day. The subway has shut down, your office has shut down, my office has shut down. We pile back into bed, under the covers — chilly air, warm bodies. Nestling and tracing the whole morning, then bundling up to walk through the empty snowdrift streets, experiencing a new kind of city quiet, then breaking it with a snowball fight. A group of teenagers joins in. We come home frozen and sweaty, botching the hot chocolate on first try, then jump back into bed for the rest of the day, emerging only to wheel over the TV and order Chinese food and check to see if the snow is still falling and falling and falling, which it is.

happenstance, *n.*

You said he wasn't even supposed to be at the convention, but one of his co-workers had gotten sick, so he was filling in at the last minute. He wasn't supposed to be at the bar when you went there with Toby, you told me. As if that in some way made it better, that fate hadn't planned it weeks in advance.

harbinger, *n.*

When I was in third grade, we would play that game at recess where you'd twist an apple while holding on to its stem, reciting the alphabet, one letter for each turn. When the stem broke, the name of your true love would be revealed.

Whenever I played, I always made sure that the apple broke at *K*. At the time I was doing this because no one in my grade had a name that began with *K*. Then, in college, it seemed like everyone I fell for was a *K*. It was enough to make me give up on the letter, and I didn't even associate it with you until later on, when I saw your signature on a credit card receipt, and the only legible letter was that first *K*.

I will admit: When I got home that night, I went to the refrigerator and took out another apple. But I stopped twisting at *J* and put the apple back.

You see, I didn't trust myself. I knew that even if the apple wasn't ready, I was going to pull that stem.

healthy, *adj.*

There are times when I'm alone that I think, *This is it. This is actually the natural state.* All I need are my thoughts and my small acts of creation and my ability to go or do whatever I want to go or do. I am myself, and that is the point. Pairing is a social construction. It is by no means necessary for everyone to do it. Maybe I'm better like this. Maybe I could live my life in my own world, and then simply leave it when it's time to go.

hiatus, *n.*

"It's up to you," you said, the graciousness of the cheater toward the cheatee.

I guess I don't believe in a small break. I feel a break is a break, and if it starts small, it only gets wider.

So I said I wanted you to stay, even though nothing could stay the same.

hubris, *n.*

Every time I call you mine, I feel like I'm forcing it, as if saying it can make it so. As if I'm reminding you, and reminding the universe: *mine.* As if that one word from me could have that kind of power.

I

I, *n.*

Me without anyone else.

idea, *n.*

"I'm quitting," you say. "I can't believe how wasted I was. This time, I'm really going to do it."

And I tell you I'll help. It's almost a script at this point.

imperceptible, *adj.*

We stopped counting our relationship in dates (first date, second date, fifth date, seventh) and started counting it in months.
That might have been the first true commitment, this shift in
terminology. We never talked about it, but we were at a party
and someone asked how long we'd been together, and when
you said, "A month and a half," I knew we had gotten there.

impromptu, *adj.*

I have summer Fridays off; you don't. So what better reason for me to take you to lunch and then keep you at lunch for the whole afternoon? Reserving these afternoons to do all the city things we never get around to doing — wandering through MoMA, stopping in at the Hayden Planetarium, hopping onto the Staten Island Ferry and riding back and forth, back and forth, watching all the people as they unknowingly parade for us. You notice clothes more than I do, so it's a pleasure to hear your running commentary, to construct lives out of worn handbags or shirts opened one button too low. Had we tried to plan these excursions, they never would have worked. There has to be that feeling of escape.

inadvertent, *adj.*

You left your email open on my computer. I couldn't help it — I didn't open any of them, but I did look at who they were from, and was relieved.

incessant, *adj.*

The doubts. You had to save me from my constant doubts. That deep-seeded feeling that I wasn't good enough for anything — I was a fake at my job, I wasn't your equal, my friends would forget me if I moved away for a month. It wasn't as easy as hearing voices — nobody was telling me this. It was just something I knew. Everyone else was playing along, but I was sure that one day they would all stop.

indelible, *adj.*

That first night, you took your finger and pointed to the top of my head, then traced a line between my eyes, down my nose, over my lips, my chin, my neck, to the center of my chest. It was so surprising, I knew I would never mimic it. That one gesture would be yours forever.

ineffable, *adj.*

These words will ultimately end up being the barest of reflections, devoid of the sensations words cannot convey. Trying to write about love is ultimately like trying to have a dictionary represent life. No matter how many words there are, there will never be enough.

infidel, *n.*

We think of them as hiding in the hills — rebels, ransack-ers, rogue revolutionaries. But really, aren't they just guilty of infidelity?

innate, *adj.*

"Why do you always make the bed?" I asked. "We're only going to get back in it later tonight."

You looked at me like I was the worst kind of slacker.

"It's just what I've always done," you said. "We always had to make our beds. Always."

integral, *adj.*

I was so nervous to meet Kathryn. You'd made it clear she was the only friend whose opinion you really cared about, so I spent more time getting dressed for her than I ever had for you. We met at that sushi place on Seventh Avenue and I awkwardly shook her hand, then told her I'd heard so much about her, which came off like me trying to legitimize your friendship, when I was the one who needed to get the stamp of approval. I was on safer ground once we started talking about books, and she seemed impressed that I actually read them. She remarked on the steadiness of my job, the steadiness of my family. I wasn't sure I wanted to be steady, but she saw my unease and assured me it was a good thing, not usually your type. We found out we'd gone to summer camp within ten minutes of each other, and that sealed it. You were lost in our tales of the Berkshires and the long, unappreciative stretches we'd spent on the Tanglewood lawn.

At the end of the dinner, I got a hug, not a handshake. She seemed so relieved. I should have been glad . . . but it only made me wonder about the other guys of yours that she'd met. I wondered why I was considered such a break from the norm.

J

jaded, *adj.*

We'll have contests to see which one of us can be more skeptical. *America will never vote for a Jew for president* right on down to *The younger, cuter, puppydog guy will totally be the next American Idol.* Like our own version of that old song — "Anything you can do, I can do bleaker."

But.

In the end, we both want the right thing to happen, the right person to win, the right idea to prevail. We have no faith that it will, but still we want it. Neither of us has given up on anything.

jerk, *v.*

"This has to stop," I say. "You have to stop hurting me. I can't take it. I really can't take it."

"I know you can't take it," you say. "But is that really my fault?"

I try to convince myself that it's the alcohol talking. But alcohol can't talk. It just sits there. It can't even get itself out of the bottle.

"It *is* your fault," I tell you. But you've already left the room.

justice, *n.*

I tell you about Sal Kinsey, the boy who spit on me every morning for a month in seventh grade, to the point that I could no longer ride the bus. It's just a story, nothing more than that. In fact, it comes up because I'm telling you how I don't really hate many people in this world, and you say that's hard to believe, and I say, "Well, there's always Sal Kinsey," and then have to explain.

The next day, you bring home a photo of him now, downloaded from the Internet. He is *morbidly obese* — one of my favorite phrases, so goth, so judgmental. He looks miserable, and the profile you've found says he's single and actively looking.

I think that will be it. But then, the next night, you tell me that you tracked down his office address. And not only that, you sent him a dozen roses, signing the card, *It is so refreshing to see that you've grown up to be fat, desperate, and lonely.* Anonymous, of course. You even ordered the bouquet online, so no florist could divulge your personal information.

I can't help but admire your capacity for creative vengeance. And at the same time, I am afraid of it.

juxtaposition, *n.*

It scares me how hard it is to remember life before you. I can't even make the comparisons anymore, because my memories of that time have all the depth of a photograph. It seems foolish to play games of *better* and *worse*. It's simply a matter of *is* and *is no longer.*

K

kerfuffle, *n.*

From now on, you are only allowed one drink at any of my office parties. One. Preferably a beer.

kinetic, *adj.*

Joanna asked me to describe you, and I said, "Kinetic."

We were both surprised by this response. Usually, with a date, it was "I don't know . . . cool" or "Not that bad" or, at the highest level of excitement, "Maybe it will work out." But there was something about you that made me think of sparks and motion.

I still see that now. Less when we're alone. More when we're with other people. When you're surrounded by life. Reaching out to it, gathering energy.

L

lackluster, *adj.*

And when Kathryn asked you about me, I imagined you said, "He's lackluster."

Which is why I waited for you to ask me out for the second date. Just to be sure I hadn't underwhelmed you.

latitude, *n.*

"We're not, like, seeing other people, right?" I asked. We were barely over the one-month mark, I believe.

You nodded.

"Excellent," I said.

"But I have to tell you something," you added — and my heart sank.

"What?"

"At first, I was seeing someone else. Only for the first week or two. Then I told him it wasn't going to work."

"Because of me?"

"Partly. And partly because it wouldn't have worked anyway."

I was glad I hadn't known I was in a contest; I don't know if I could have handled that. But still, it was strange, to realize my version of those weeks was so far from yours.

What a strange phrase — *not seeing other people*. As if it's been constructed to be a lie. We see other people all the time. The question is what we do about it.

leery, *adj.*

Those first few weeks, after you told me, I wasn't sure we were going to make it. After working for so long on being sure of each other, sure of this thing, suddenly we were unsure again. I didn't know whether or not to touch you, sleep with you, have sex with you.

Finally, I said, "It's over."

libidinous, *adj.*

I never understood why anyone would have sex on the floor.
Until I was with you and I realized: you don't ever realize
you're on the floor.

livid, *adj.*

Fuck you for cheating on me. Fuck you for reducing it to the word *cheating*. As if this were a card game, and you sneaked a look at my hand. Who came up with the term *cheating*, anyway? A cheater, I imagine. Someone who thought *liar* was too harsh. Someone who thought *devastator* was too emotional. The same person who thought, oops, he'd gotten *caught with his hand in the cookie jar*. Fuck you. This isn't about slipping yourself an extra twenty dollars of Monopoly money. These are our lives. You went and broke our lives. You are so much worse than a cheater. You killed something. And you killed it when its back was turned.

love, *n.*

I'm not going to even try.

lover, *n.*

Oh, how I hated this word. So pretentious, like it was always being translated from the French. The tint and taint of illicit, illegitimate affections. Dictionary meaning: *a person having a love affair.* Impermanent. Unfamilial. Inextricably linked to sex.

I have never wanted a lover. In order to have a lover, I must go back to the root of the word. For I have never wanted a lover, but I have always wanted to love, and to be loved.

There is no word for the recipient of the love. There is only a word for the giver. There is the assumption that lovers come in pairs.

When I say, *Be my lover,* I don't mean, *Let's have an affair.* I don't mean, *Sleep with me.* I don't mean, *Be my secret.*

I want us to go back down to that root.

I want you to be the one who loves me.

I want to be the one who loves you.

M

macabre, *adj.*

If you ever need proof that I love you, the fact that I allowed you to dress me up as a dead baby Jesus for Halloween should do it. Although I suppose it would be even better proof if it hadn't been Halloween.

makeshift, *adj.*

I had always thought there were two types of people: the help-less and the fixers. Since I'd always been in the first group, call-ing my landlord whenever the faucet dripped, I was hoping you'd be a fixer. But once we moved in together, I realized there's a third group: the inventors. You possess only a vague notion of how to fix things, but that doesn't stop you from using bubble gum as a sealant, or trying to create ouchless mousetraps out of peanut-butter crackers, a hollowed-out Dustbuster, and a pic-ture of a scarecrow torn out of a magazine fashion spread.

Things rarely get fixed the way they need to be.

masochist, *n.*

If there wasn't a word for it, would we realize our masochism
as much?

meander, *v.*

". . . because when it all comes down to it, there's no such thing as a two-hit wonder. So it's better just to have that one song that everyone knows, instead of diluting it with a follow-up that only half succeeds. I mean, who really cares what Soft Cell's next single was, as long as we have 'Tainted Love'?"

I stop. You're still listening.

"Wait," I say. "What was I talking about? How did we get to 'Tainted Love'?"

"Let's see," you say. "I believe we started roughly at the Democratic gains in the South, then jumped back to the election of 1948, dipping briefly into northern constructions of the South, vis-à-vis *Steel Magnolias*, *Birth of a Nation*, Johnny Cash, and *Fried Green Tomatoes*. Which landed you on *To Kill a Mockingbird*, and how it is both Southern and universal, which — correct me if I'm wrong — got us to Harper Lee and her lack of a follow-up novel, intersected with the theory, probably wrong, that Truman Capote wrote the novel, then hopping over to literary one-hit wonders, and using musical one-hit wonders to make a point about their special place in our culture. I think."

"Thank you," I say. "That's wonderful."

misgivings, *n.*

Last night, I got up the courage to ask you if you regretted us.

    "There are things I miss," you said. "But if I didn't have you, I'd miss more."

motif, *n.*

You don't love me as much as I love you. You don't love me as much as I love you. You don't love me as much as I love you.

N

narcissism, *n.*

You couldn't believe I didn't own a full-length mirror.

nascent, *adj.*

"I just don't like babies," you said as I led you home.

"Now is probably not the time for this conversation," I told you.

"Whatever. I'm just saying. I really don't like babies. You should know that. I don't want to keep that from you."

"We've actually had this conversation," I said. "And also conversations where you say how great kids are. But the last time we had this specific conversation, it was after Lila's kid threw up on you."

I should not have mentioned it. You paused for a moment and I thought, *Lord, please don't puke now, just to illustrate a point.*

But you recovered.

"I'm just saying. I really can't stand babies."

I should have let it go. But instead I asked, "But don't you want to pass on your incredible genes?"

neophyte, *n.*

There are millions upon millions of people who have been
through this before — why is it that no one can give me good
advice?

nomenclature, *n.*

You got up to stretch, and I said, "Hey, you're in Ivan's way."

You looked at the TV and said, "That's Tina Fey."

I tried to keep a straight face when I explained, "No. The TV's name is Ivan."

"The TV has a name."

"Yes. And you'll never guess what it is."

"Does everything have a name?"

The answer was no, only Ivan. Because when I bought it with Joanna, I promised her I would call it Ivan.

But I didn't tell you that. Instead, I told you I'd named everything.

You pointed to the couch.

"Olga," I said.

The refrigerator.

"Calvin."

The kitchen table.

"Selena."

The bed.

"Otis," I said. "The bed is named Otis."

You pointed to the light fixture over our head.

"C'mon," I said. "Who names a light fixture?"

non sequitur, *n.*

This is what it sounds like when doves cry.

obstinate, *adj.*

Sometimes it becomes a contest: Which is more stubborn, the love or the two arguing people caught within it?

offshoot, *n.*

"I don't like Vampire Weekend nearly as much as Kathryn does," you said. "Ask her to go with you."

And so we went on our first date without you — awkward, hesitant, self-conscious. The best friend and the boyfriend — no way to know how to split the check. To talk about you would be disloyal, weird. But what else did we have in common?

Oh, yes. Vampire Weekend.

But halfway through the meal I said something she found funny, and when she laughed, I had to say, "Wow, you two have the same laugh. Did one of you get it from the other, or have you always laughed like that?" And we were off. She said she hoped I was more successful in sharing a bed with you than she had been on your junior year road trip, when you would take up all the space and snore so loudly that one night she went and slept in the bathtub. You didn't notice, and the next morning you turned on the shower without noticing she was inside. She still didn't know who screamed louder. And I told her about the time that I got so tired of you stealing the sheets that in my sleep-weary logic I decided the thing to do was to tie them around my legs, knot and all, and how, when you attempted to steal them that night, you ended yanking me into you, and I was so startled that I sprang up, tripped, and was nearly concussed.

"That's how you end up when you're with our dear one," she said wryly. "Nearly concussed."

It wasn't like we held hands during the concert. We didn't go out for wine or shots or milkshakes afterwards. But I liked that she was no longer entirely yours. We had four hours of history without you.

only, *adj.*

That's the dilemma, isn't it? When you're single, there's the sadness and joy of *only me*. And when you're paired, there's the sadness and joy of *only you*.

paleontology, *n.*

You couldn't believe the longest relationship I'd ever been in had only lasted for five months.

"Ever?" you asked, as if I might have overlooked a marriage.

I couldn't say, "I never found anyone who interested me all that much," because it was only our second date, and the jury was still hearing your case.

I sat there as you excavated your boyfriends, laid the bones out on the table for me to see. I shifted them around, tried to reassemble them, if only to see if they bore any resemblance to me.

panoply, *n.*

We stuck to the plan: you had your bookshelves and I had mine. Yours simply had books, most of them from college, while mine was overrun by souvenir thimbles purchased by my pre-teen self, compact discs that had been orphaned from their cases, mugs from colleges attended by forgotten friends, and jam jars of quarters (just in case, for some reason, I had to quickly launder everything we owned).

You never seemed to mind. Although one day you did say, "If our shelves were a seesaw, my things would be stuck in the air."

I didn't know whether you were being judgmental or self-pitying. But I *had* learned: there's no good answer to either.

peregrinations, *n.*

I'd never had to teach someone how to travel before. Drugging you up for the airplane, dragging you hither and thither through Montreal, Seattle, San Francisco. Your parents never took you on trips as a kid, not when they were together and not when they were apart, and I think this left your sense of exploration stunted. At least, that's my theory. Eventually I won you over to the geography of wandering. Although I will admit that for you the best part is still the napping in the middle of the day.

perfunctory, *adj.*

I get to sign some of your Christmas cards, but others I don't.

persevere, *v.*

Those first few weeks, after you told me, I wasn't sure we were going to make it. After working for so long on being sure of each other, sure of this thing, suddenly we were unsure again. I didn't know whether or not to touch you, sleep with you, have sex with you.

Finally, I said, "It's over."

You started to cry, and I quickly said, "No — I mean this part is over. We have to get to the next part."

placid, *adj.*

Sometimes I love it when we just lie on our backs, gaze off, stay still.

posterity, *n.*

I try not to think about us growing old together, mostly because I try not to think about growing old at all. Both things — the years passing, the years together — are too enormous to contemplate. But one morning, I gave in. You were asleep, and I imagined you older and older. Your hair graying, your skin folded and creased, your breath catching. And I found myself thinking: If this continues, if this goes on, then when I die, your memories of me will be my greatest accomplishment. Your memories will be my most lasting impression.

punctuate, *v.*

Cue the imaginary interviewer:

Q: So when all is said and done, what have you learned here?

A: The key to a successful relationship isn't just in the words, it's in the choice of punctuation. When you're in love with someone, a well-placed question mark can be the difference between bliss and disaster, and a deeply respected period or a cleverly inserted ellipsis can prevent all kinds of exclamations.

qualm, *n.*

There is no reason to make fun of me for flossing twice a day.

quintessence, *n.*

It's the way you say thank you like you're genuinely thankful. I have never met anyone else who does that on a regular basis.

quixotic, *adj.*

Finally, I said, "It's over."

You started to cry, and I quickly said, "No — I mean this part is over. We have to get to the next part."

And you said, "I'm not sure we can."

rapprochement, *n.*

I remember my grandmother saying, "You have to let the cake cool before you frost it."

raze, *v.*

It sounded like you were lifting me, but it all fell.

recant, *v.*

I want to take back at least half of the "I love you"s, because I didn't mean them as much as the other ones. I want to take back the book of artsy photos I gave you, because you didn't get it and said it was hipster trash. I want to take back what I said about you being an emotional zombie. I want to take back the time I called you "honey" in front of your sister and you looked like I had just shown her pictures of us having sex. I want to take back the wineglass I broke when I was mad, because it was a nice wineglass and the argument would have ended anyway. I want to take back the time we had sex in a rent-a-car, not because I feel bad about the people who got the car after us, but because it was massively uncomfortable. I want to take back the trust I had while you were away in Austin. I want to take back the time I said you were a genius, because I was being sarcastic and I should have just said you'd hurt my feelings. I want to take back the secrets I told you so I can decide now whether to tell them to you again. I want to take back the piece of me that lies in you, to see if I truly miss it. I want to take back at least half the "I love you"s, because it feels safer that way.

reservation, *n.*

There are times when I worry that I've already lost myself. That is, that my self is so inseparable from being with you that if we were to separate, I would no longer be. I save this thought for when I feel the darkest discontent. I never meant to depend so much on someone else.

rest, *v.* and *n.*

Rest with me for the rest of this.
    That's it. Come closer.
    We're here.

retrospective, *n.*

I catch you checking out some guy on the street. This is no big deal, because we both like to look at other people when we're walking around. But this time it's not an observational thrill on your face. You notice me noticing, and you say, "He just looked like someone I know."

A week later, we're going through photographs, and there he is, hiking through Appalachia with you. It wasn't him on the street, but it was definitely him on your mind. I wonder why you said "someone I know" instead of "someone I knew."

Two days after that, I'm walking along alone, and I see someone who looks like the someone who reminded you of him. I feel the irrational desire to pull this stranger aside and make sure he doesn't know you.

reverberate, *v.*

Why did your father leave?

rifle, *v.*

You told me to get the money for the pizza from your wallet. So I had permission, I swear. You were five dollars short, but your driver's license photo was worth me making up the difference. And then I found the photo behind your health insurance card: you and me in front of the bay in San Francisco. I remember you stopping that woman and asking her to take the picture, and how she had no idea how to use the camera on your phone. You gave her the full tutorial as she oohed and aahed. I stood there in the wind, shifting from foot to foot as the photographer counseled the assistant, and all I could think was that I should have been the one with the camera, because the two of you were such a funny picture. Instead, we have this blurry, happy shot, which must mean something to you if you carry it around like this, folded to fit.

rubberneck, *v.*

It's not only car accidents. Why is it only car accidents? It can also be when I lean over you in the morning, trying to see through the sliver of open window shade to find out what the weather is like. Cranes, the birds with the rubber necks, don't always find carnage. Sometimes it's just rain.

S

sacrosanct, *adj.*

The nape of your neck. Even the sound of the word *nape* sounds holy to me. That and the hollow of your neck, the peek of your chest that your shirt sometimes reveals. These are the stations of my quietest, most insistent desire.

sartorial, *adj.*

"I'm so tired of those slippers," you said.

I shook my head, and you had the nerve to say, "Well, that's not very nice."

And I explained, "I'm not laughing at you. I'm laughing at your unintentional quoting of Hedda Gabler."

"You want to see Hedda Gabler?" you asked. Then you threw my slippers in the fire.

It escalated. I lunged for the hideous scarf your great-aunt had sent you — it would have been spared had she knitted it herself, but I suspected foreign sweatshop labor. You retaliated by burning my "sleeping T-shirt" (*American Idiot* tour), a patchwork of stains and holes. I topped that with your unbearable tennis sneakers — until the rubber started to burn, and the smell made us stop.

"I loved those slippers," I said.

"I assure you," you said, "they did not love you back."

scapegoat, *n.*

I think our top two are:

    1. Not enough coffee.
    2. Too much coffee.

serrated, *adj.*

And you said, "I'm not sure we can."

solipsistic, *adj.*

Go ahead, I thought. *Go ahead. Go ahead.* I got stuck there. *Go ahead. Go ahead.* Because I genuinely couldn't see anything after that.

sonnet, *n.*

(NOTE ON THE LEAP: How rough and worn the weight
of flight — the soul, when gathered, forms its own
twinned claw and wing, each severed arc, the nape —
all grown inside the body, left. Alone with loss, life
rises: emblazoned air, trembling star of made
faith. The fall that forms in the gut blooms in the
arms before the mind, remembering how dangerous
and hard the world is when shut, opens its doors
so air can cool what light arrives. The chest
unhinges, strong from panic, and the loch that
is the heart begins to fit. The wind grows
sturdier, its skin gigantic. The room that was
the source becomes the field, opening out,
the stage a hoard revealed.)

— *Billy Merrell*, The Proposals

stanchion, *n.*

I don't want to be the strong one, but I don't want to be the weak one, either. Why does it feel like it's always one or the other? When we embrace, one of us is always holding the other a little tighter.

stymie, *v.*

That ten-letter word for *moderate in eating or drinking* —
first letter *a*, fourth letter *t*? I knew it all along, but was so
entertained by your frustration that I kept it to myself.

suffuse, *v.*

I don't like it when you use my shampoo, because then your hair smells like me, not you.

sunder, *v.*

Nobody ever told us, "Save it for the bedroom." But isn't that what we do? All those times you've wanted to strike me — by which I mean, all those times I've wanted to strike you — haven't we translated it into the shove and twist, the scratch and press, the capture and hold? There are times when I look in your eyes and realize you mean it. We've lost track of the game. We're communicating in earnest now, all the things we'd never say.

T

tableau, *n.*

We go to visit two friends who've been together for ten years now, five times longer than we have. I look at the ease with which they sit together on the couch. They joke with each other, get annoyed with each other, curl into each other like apostrophes within a quotation mark as they talk. I realize that two years is not a long time. I realize that even ten years is not a long time. But when it seems insurmountable, I need reminders like this that you can get used to it. That it can take on the comfort of the right choice. That lasting things do, in fact, last.

taciturn, *adj.*

There are days you come home silent. You say words, but you're still silent. I used to bombard you with conversational crowbars, but now I simply let the apartment fall mute. I hear you in the room — turning on music, typing on the keys, getting up for a drink, shifting in your chair. I try to have my conversation with those sounds.

tenet, *n.*

At the end of the French movie, the lover sings, "Love me less, but love me for a long time."

transient, *adj.*

In school, the year was the marker. Fifth grade. Senior year of high school. Sophomore year of college. Then after, the jobs were the marker. That office. This desk. But now that school is over and I've been working at the same place in the same office at the same desk for longer than I can truly believe, I realize: You have become the marker. This is your era. And it's only if it goes on and on that I will have to look for other ways to identify the time.

traverse, *v.*

You started to cry, and I quickly said, "No — I mean this part is over. We have to get to the next part."

And you said, "I'm not sure we can."

Without even having to think about it, I replied, "Of course we can."

"How can you be so sure?" you asked.

And I said, "I'm sure. Isn't that enough?"

trenchant, *adj.*

You never let things go unanswered for too long. Emails. Phone calls. Questions. As if you know the waiting is the hardest part for me.

U

ubiquitous, *adj.*

When it's going well, the fact of it is everywhere. It's there in the song that shuffles into your ears. It's there in the book you're reading. It's there on the shelves of the store as you reach for a towel and forget about the towel. It's there as you open the door. As you stare off on the subway, it's what you're looking at. You wear it on the inside of your hat. It lines your pockets. It's the temperature.

The hitch, of course, is that when it's going badly, it's in all the same places.

unabashedly, *adv.*

We were walking home late from a bar — and the term *walking* is used loosely here, because you were doing something between a skip and a stumble — and suddenly you started singing out your love for me. My name and everything, loud enough to reach the top floors of all the buildings. I should have told you to stop, but I didn't want you to stop. I didn't mind if your love for me woke people up. I didn't mind if it somehow sneaked into their sleep.

You grabbed my hand and twirled me around, two sidewalk sweethearts. Then, very earnestly, you stopped, leaned over, and whispered, "You know, I'd get a tattoo with your name on it. Only, I want you to have the freedom to change your name if you want to."

I thanked you, and you resumed your song.

vagary, *n.*

The mistake is thinking there can be an antidote to the uncertainty.

vestige, *n.*

The night after we decided to move in together, we stayed over at my apartment. I looked at the things on my walls — the unframed posters from MoMA, the Doisneau kiss that had followed me from college, the album covers with push pins pressing into their corners. I had never had any desire to change anything, but suddenly I knew it was all going to change. I knew that when it came time to roll them up or pack them away, they would never be seen again.

I told you this, and you suggested that we go for a beginning instead of two continuations. Why try to angle together the wall souvenirs of our new-to-New-York lives, when we could invent new hieroglyphs to represent us? The lamp could stay and the lime-green couch could continue to park itself in front of the TV, but the postcards would be mailed into drawers and the wreath my mother sent last Christmas would be shown another door.

And this is what happened. We both took it as an opportunity to peel the wallpaper from our lives. The only thing I kept out were the photographs of my friends and family, placed on a wall with photographs of your friends and (less so) family on the other end, as if they were meeting for the first time, still too shy or wary to mingle.

viable, *adj.*

I'll go for a drink with friends after work, and even though I have you, I still want to be desirable. I'll fix my hair as if it's a date. I'll check out the room along with everyone else. If someone comes to flirt with me, I will flirt back, but only up to a point. You have nothing to worry about — it never gets further than the question about where I live. And in New York, that's usually the second or third question. But for that first question, where it still seems like it might be possible, I look for that confirmation that if I didn't have you, I'd still be a person someone would want.

voluminous, *adj.*

I have already spent roughly five thousand hours asleep next to you. This has to mean something.

wane, *v.*

The week before our first anniversary, I thought, *I can't do this anymore.* I was shopping with Joanna, shopping for you, and suddenly I couldn't stay in the store. She asked me what was wrong, and I told her I had to end it. She was surprised, and asked me why I thought so. I told her it wasn't a thought, more a feeling, like I couldn't breathe and knew I had to get some air. It was a survival instinct, I told her.

She said it was time for dinner. Then she sat me down and told me not to worry. She said moments like this were like waking up in the middle of the night: You're scared, you're disoriented, and you're completely convinced you're right. But then you stay awake a little longer and you realize things aren't as fearful as they seem.

"You're breathing," she said.

We sat there. I breathed.

whet, *v.*

You kiss me when you get home, and when I kiss you back
longer, harder, you say, "Later, dear. Later."

woo, *v.*

I told you that it was ridiculous to pay thirty dollars for a dozen roses on Valentine's Day. I forbade you to do it.

So that day, when I went to pay for lunch, what did I find? In my wallet, thirty singles, each with roses printed on it. I imagined you feeding them through your color printer. Oh, the smile that must have played across your face. I had to ask the woman behind the counter to take a quick picture of my own smile, to send it right back to you.

X

x, *n.*

Doesn't it strike you as strange that we have a letter in the alphabet that nobody uses? It represents one-twenty-sixth of the possibility of our language, and we let it languish. If you and I really, truly wanted to change the world, we'd invent more words that started with *x*.

Y

yarn, *n.*

Maybe language is kind, giving us these double meanings. Maybe it's trying to teach us a lesson, that we can always be two things at once.

Knit me a sweater out of your best stories. Not the day's petty injustices. Not the glimmer of a seven-eighths-forgotten moment from your past. Not something that somebody said to somebody, who then told it to you. No, I want a yarn. It doesn't have to be true.

"Okay," you say. "Do you want to know how I met you?"

I nod.

"It was on the carousel. You were on the pink horse, I was on the yellow. You were two horses ahead of me, and from the moment you got in the saddle, I wanted to draw up right next to you and say hello.

"Around and around we went, and I kept waiting for my horse to pull ahead. I sensed it would know when I was ready, and it was waiting for that moment. You rose and you fell, and I followed, and I followed. I thought my chance would never come. But then, like magic, all the power in the entire city went out at once. It was darkness, utter darkness. The music stopped, and there were only heartbeats to be heard. Heartbeats. I couldn't see you, and worried that you'd left. But right at that moment, the moon came out from behind the clouds. And there you were. I stepped off my horse just as you stepped off yours. I turned right and you turned left. We met in the middle."

"And what did you say?"

"Don't you remember? I said, 'What a lovely evening this is.' And you said, 'I was just thinking the same thing.' "

As long as we can conjure, who needs anything else? As long as we can agree on the magical lie and be happy, what more is there to ask for?

"I loved you from that moment on," I say.

"I loved you from that moment on," you agree.

yearning, *n.* and *adj.*

At the core of this desire is the belief that everything can be perfect.

yell, *v.*

I found myself thinking of our verbal exchanges in terms of the verbs we'd use to transcribe them. Every time I came up with *said*, I knew we were okay. *Asked* or *replied* — shakier ground. Even *joked* could be dicey. And *yelled* — that meant trouble. *Shouted* could mean that the other person was simply too far away to hear. But *yelled* — that meant the boiling point.

Our apartment didn't have any good doors to slam. If you wanted to slam a door, you would either end up in the hallway or trapped in the bathroom. Those were the only options.

yesterday, *n.*

You called to ask me when I was coming home, and when I reminded you that I wasn't coming home, you sounded so disappointed that I decided to come home.

Z

zenith, *n.*

I'm standing in the bathroom, drying my hands on your towel, and you're hovering in the kitchen. I am happy from dinner, happy the day is over, and before I can ask you what's going on, you tell me there's something we need to talk about.

This is it, the moment before you tell me the precise thing I don't want to know.

Is this the zenith? This last moment of ignorance?

Or does it come much later?

acknowledgments

I would like to thank all of my friends who read an earlier form of this book as a story I gave them for Valentine's Day. In particular, I would like to thank Billy Merrell, Ann Martin, John Green, Eliot Schrefer, and Dan Ehrenhaft, whose reaction to the story made me believe in it enough to take it further.

Thank you to Bill Clegg and Jonathan Galassi for helping me to make this book everything it could be. Thanks also to Jesse Coleman, Shaun Dolan, Alicia Gordon, and everyone else at FSG and WMEE, as well as the book's foreign publishers, whose enthusiasm is deeply appreciated.

Finally, thanks to my various families. My family of friends. My family of YA authors. My family at Scholastic. And, most of all, my real family—Mom, Dad, Adam, Jennifer, Paige, Matthew, Hailey. It's so much more meaningful to have you share this with me.